LIGHTS FOR GITA

by Rachna Gilmore

Illustrated by Alice Priestley

Tilbury House, Publishers
Gardiner, Maine

W9-AXZ-052

Gita pulled her hat down over her ears as she stepped off the school bus.

"Divali," she whispered. "Today's really and truly Divali."

But nothing in the November gloom seemed like Divali.

Somehow, moving here for Papa's new job no longer seemed an exciting adventure.

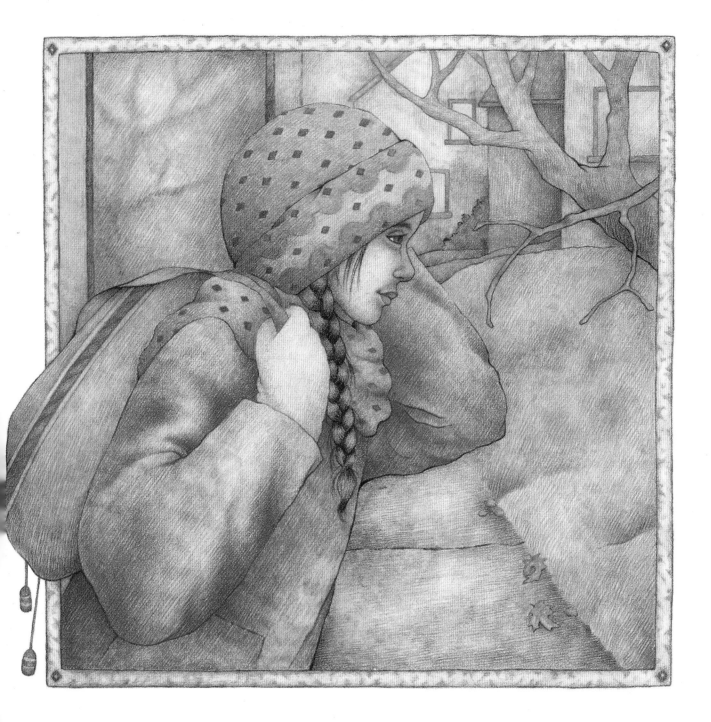

Today, New Delhi would be glowing with celebration. All her aunts, uncles, and cousins would be together at her grandparents' house. They'd be laughing, talking, and exchanging sweets with friends and neighbours. In the evening they'd light *diyas* to honour the Goddess Lakshmi who brought prosperity and happiness. And then — fireworks. The whole city would be brilliant with fireworks.

Gita looked anxiously at the dark clouds.

"Please, *please* don't rain."

Papa had said, "I'll be home early — with fireworks for our first Divali in our new home."

It wouldn't be like Divali at her grandparents'. Still, Mummy had made their favourite sweets — golden *perras*, spiral *jallebies* — and she'd let Gita invite five school friends to help celebrate. Gita had wanted to invite her whole class, but you had to be quiet in an apartment.

Not outside, though. Fireworks, lots of them — that's what Divali was all about, the Festival of Lights.

Gita glared at the grey sky before racing up the creaky stairs to their apartment.

She flung her arms around her mother. Papa was home early, just as he'd promised.

"Did you get the fireworks, Papa?"

"Yes, I got them," he said slowly. "But Gita, Divali isn't just fireworks. There's … "

"Show me, Papa, where are they?"

Gently, Papa turned Gita towards the window. A large drop splashed against the glass. Then another and another.

"It won't last long," said Gita, her voice wobbly.

"The forecast says freezing rain tonight," said Papa. "Never mind. We'll have the fireworks tomorrow."

"But I promised my friends … "

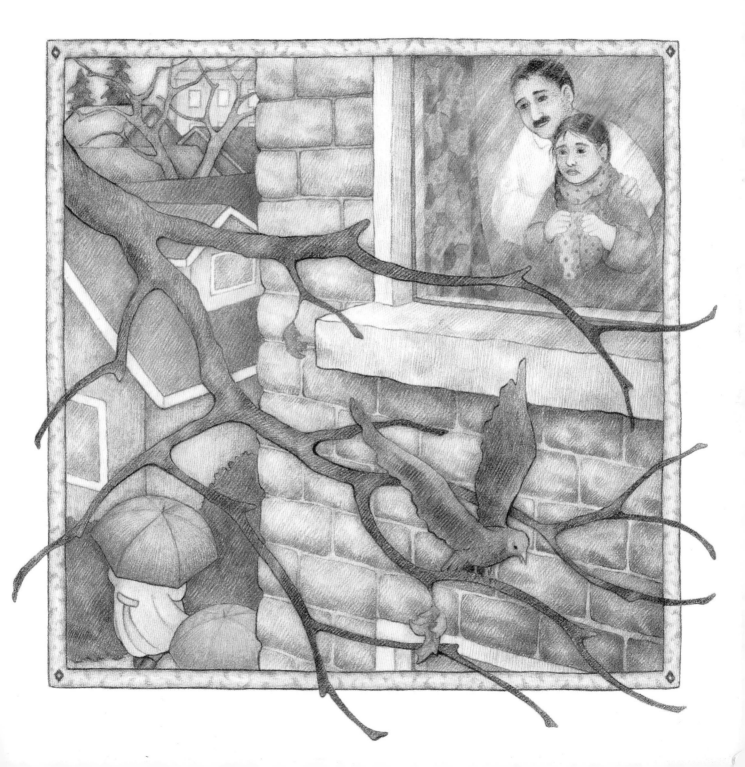

"We'll turn on all the lights," said Mummy. "And light the *diyas*. You and your friends will have a lovely party."

Gita blinked back her tears.

"Come," said her mother. "Change into your new dress. Then we'll light the *diyas*."

Gita and her mother set the little clay pots along the windowsills and around the room. Needles of ice stung the windows. Freezing rain on Divali! How could such a place ever be home?

Last year Divali had been warm and joyful. She and her cousins had startled everyone with noisy crackers called *little rascals*. They'd whispered in the prayer room as the incense smoke curled upwards and the grown-ups chanted. Grandmother had told them stories of Prince Ram and his wife Sita and of their homecoming on Divali. And in the evening! Cones spouted fountains of fire, Catherine wheels whirled, and hissing rockets burst into dazzling showers of colour.

A sudden gust rattled the window. Gita stuck out her tongue. *You can't get in! And you won't spoil my party!* She gave a hard twist to the wisps of cotton wick.

Mummy, bangles tinkling, filled the *diyas* with mustard oil. As she finished, the phone rang.

Gita heard the murmur of her mother's voice, the click of the receiver, and then more ringing.

She shook the box of matches impatiently as her mother came back. "Can I light the first one?"

Mummy just smiled and smoothed Gita's hair.

"That was Jennie and Helga. It's too icy to drive, they can't come."

The phone rang again.

Gita ran to her room. She burrowed into bed, and jerked the covers over her head. "I *hate* this place," she sobbed.

Mummy lifted back the covers and gently hugged Gita.

"Amy hasn't called. And she does live nearby."

Gita pulled away and blew her nose.

"Gita," said Mummy softly. "Divali is really about filling the darkness with light. Fireworks can't do it for us. We must do it ourselves." Mummy's smile was bright, but also sad — like grandmother's smile when they'd said goodbye.

For a long moment Gita sat still. Then she managed a watery smile. "Let's light the *diyas*."

One by one, golden flames quivered and sprang to life. The warm fragrance of mustard oil filled the room.

Just as Gita lit the last wick the electric lights flickered — on, off, on again. Then all the lights — in the apartment, in all the houses, even the street lamps — died.

Darkness on Divali! Gita's throat tightened.

Then she began to laugh.

In the sudden rush of darkness their *diyas* glowed — bright, brighter, brightest — filling the living room with light.

"We beat the darkness, we beat the darkness!" Gita clapped her hands.

"Lakshmi will come for sure. We'll have wonderful luck," said Mummy.

Gita ran to the window. The *diyas'* reflection made it seem as if there were another shining room outside. She sang softly. Drops of freezing rain glittered as they flew past.

Slowly, the headlights of a car came down the street and stopped in front of their building.

"It's Amy!" shouted Gita.

Papa started downstairs with the flashlight. Gita ran ahead in the bouncing circle of light. She opened the front door.

"Careful, it's icy," called Papa.

Gita took a few cautious steps. She stopped, eyes wide.

The whole world glistened! The sidewalks, every branch, every twig, the lamp post, even the blades of grass!

In the dark city, only their windows blazed with the steady glow of *diyas*. The ice, reflecting their light, sparkled and danced like fireworks.

Amy's voice brought her back. "Gita, tomorrow we can go sliding. It'll be like flying."

Gita's eyes shone. She'd have to write her grandparents about this Divali in her new home. "Hey,
Amy, let's play hide and seek while the power's still
out."

She took one last look at the light singing in the
heart of the ice. "Come on," she shouted, "race you
upstairs!"